Nathaniel Hawthorne

Colonial Stories

Nathaniel Hawthorne

Colonial Stories

ISBN/EAN: 9783744750004

Printed in Europe, USA, Canada, Australia, Japan

Cover: Foto ©Andreas Hilbeck / pixelio.de

More available books at **www.hansebooks.com**

COLONIAL STORIES

BY

NATHANIEL HAWTHORNE

ILLUSTRATED BY

FRANK T. MERRILL

BOSTON
L. C. PAGE AND COMPANY
(INCORPORATED)
1897

List of Illustrations

by
Frank T. Merrill.

ILLUSTRATIONS.

ILLUSTRATIONS.

Howes Masqverade.

y^e Province House.

COLONIAL STORIES.

I.

HOWE'S MASQUERADE.

AFTERNOON, last summer, while walking along Washington Street, my eye was attracted by a sign-board protruding over a narrow archway nearly opposite the Old South Church. The sign represented the front of a stately edifice, which was designated as the "OLD PROVINCE HOUSE, kept by Thomas Waite." I was glad to be thus reminded of a purpose, long entertained, of visiting and rambling over the mansion of the old royal governors of Massachusetts; and entering the arched passage, which penetrated through the middle of a brick row of shops, a few steps transported me from the busy heart of modern Boston into a small and secluded court-yard. One side of this space was occupied by the square front of the Province House, three stories high, and surmounted by a cupola, on the top of which a gilded Indian was discernible with his bow bent and his arrow on the string, as if aiming at the weathercock on the spire of the Old South. The figure has kept this attitude for seventy years or more, ever since good Deacon Drowne, a cunning carver of wood, first stationed him on his long sentinel's watch over the city.

The Province House is constructed of brick, which seems recently to have been overlaid with a coat of light-colored paint. A flight of red freestone steps, fenced in by a balustrade of curiously wrought iron, ascends from the courtyard to the spacious porch, over which is a balcony, with an iron balustrade of similar pattern and workmanship to that beneath. These letters and figures — 16 P.S. 79 — are wrought into the iron-work of the balcony, and probably express the date of the edifice, with the initials of its founder's name. A wide door with double leaves admitted me into the hall or entry, on the right of which is the entrance to the bar-room.

It was in this apartment, I presume, that the ancient governors held their levees, with vice-regal pomp, surrounded by the military men, the councillors, the judges, and other officers of the crown, while all the loyalty of the province thronged to do them honor. But the room, in its present condition, cannot boast even of faded magnificence. The panelled wainscot is covered with dingy paint, and acquires a duskier hue from the deep shadow into which the Province House is thrown by the brick block that shuts it in from Washington Street. A ray of sunshine never visits this apartment any more than the glare of the festal torches which have been extinguished from the era

"The story of each blue tile

of the Revolution. The most venerable and ornamental object is a chimney-piece set round with Dutch tiles of blue-figured china, representing scenes from Scripture; and, for aught I know, the lady of Pownall or Bernard may have sat beside this fireplace, and told her children the story of each blue tile. A bar in modern style, well replenished with decanters, bottles, cigar-boxes, and network bags of lemons, and provided with a beer-pump and a soda-fount, extends along one side of the room. At my entrance, an elderly person was smacking his lips, with a zest which satisfied me that the cellars of the Province House still hold good liquor, though doubtless of other vintages than were quaffed by the old governors. After sipping a glass of port sangaree, prepared by the skilful hands of Mr. Thomas Waite, I besought that worthy successor and representative of so many historic personages to conduct me over their time-honored mansion.

He readily complied ; but, to confess the truth, I was forced to draw strenuously upon my imagination, in order to find aught that was interesting in a house which, without its historic associations, would have seemed merely such a tavern as is usually favored by the custom of decent city boarders and old-fashioned country gentlemen. The chambers, which were probably spacious in former times, are now cut up by partitions, and subdivided into little nooks, each affording scanty room for the narrow bed and chair and dressing-table of a single lodger. The great staircase, however, may be termed, without much hyperbole, a feature of grandeur and magnificence. It winds through the midst of the house by flights of broad steps, each flight terminating in a square landing-place, whence the ascent is continued towards the cupola. A carved balustrade, freshly painted in the lower stories, but growing dingier as we ascend, borders the staircase with its quaintly twisted and intertwined pillars, from top to bottom. Up these stairs the military boots, or perchance the gouty shoes, of many a governor have trodden, as the wearers mounted to the cupola, which afforded them so wide a view over their metropolis and the surrounding country. The cupola is an octagon, with several windows, and a door opening upon the roof. From this station, as I pleased myself with imagining, Gage may have beheld his disastrous victory on Bunker Hill (unless one of the tri-mountains intervened), and Howe have marked the approaches of Washington's besieging army; although the buildings, since erected in the vicinity, have shut out almost every object, save the steeple of the Old South, which seems almost within arm's-length. Descending from the cupola, I paused in the garret to observe the ponderous white-oak framework, so much more massive than the frames of modern houses, and thereby resembling an antique skeleton. The brick walls, the materials of which were imported from Holland, and the timbers of the mansion, are still as sound as ever; but the floors and other interior parts being greatly

decayed, it is contemplated to gut the whole, and build a new house within the ancient frame and brick work. Among other inconveniences of the present edifice, mine host mentioned that any jar or motion was apt to shake down the dust of ages out of the ceiling of one chamber upon the floor of that beneath it.

We stepped forth from the great front window into the balcony, where, in old times, it was doubtless the custom of the king's representative to show himself to a loyal populace, requiting their huzzas and tossed-up hats with stately bendings of his dignified person. In those days, the front of the Province House looked upon the street; and the whole site now occupied by the brick range of stores, as well as the

present court-yard, was laid out in grass-plats, overshadowed by trees and bordered by a wrought-iron fence. Now, the old aristocratic edifice hides its time-worn visage behind an upstart modern building. At one of the back windows I observed some pretty tailoresses, sewing, and chatting, and laughing, with now and then a careless glance towards the balcony. Descending thence, we again entered the bar-room, where the elderly gentleman above mentioned, the smack of whose lips had spoken so favorably for Mr. Waite's good liquor, was still lounging in his chair. He seemed to be, if not a lodger, at least a familiar

visitor of the house, who might be supposed to have his regular score at the bar, his summer seat at the open window, and his prescriptive corner at the winter's fireside. Being of a sociable aspect, I ventured to address him with a remark, calculated to draw forth his historical reminiscences, if any such were in his mind; and it gratified me to discover, that, between memory and tradition, the old gentleman was really possessed of some very pleasant gossip about the Province House. The portion of his talk which chiefly interested me was the outline of the following legend. He professed to have received it at one or two removes from an eye-witness; but this derivation, together with the lapse of time, must have afforded opportunities for many variations of the narrative; so that despairing of literal and absolute truth, I have not scrupled to make such further changes as seemed conducive to the reader's profit and delight.

At one of the entertainments given at the Province House, during the latter part of the siege of Boston, there passed a scene which has never yet been satisfactorily explained. The officers of the British army, and the loyal gentry of the province, most of whom were collected within the beleaguered town, had been invited to a masked ball; for it was the policy of Sir William Howe to hide the distress and danger of the period, and the desperate aspect of the siege, under an ostentation of festivity. The spectacle of this evening, if the oldest members of the provincial court circle might be believed, was the most gay and gorgeous affair that had· occurred in the annals of the government. The brilliantly lighted apartments were thronged with figures that seemed to have stepped from the dark canvas of historic portraits, or to have flitted forth from the magic pages of romance, or at least to have flown hither from one of the London theatres, without a change of garments. Steeled knights of the Conquest, bearded statesmen of Queen Elizabeth, and high-ruffled ladies of her court, were mingled with charac-

ters of comedy, such as a party-colored Merry Andrew, jingling his cap and bells; a Falstaff, almost as provocative of laughter as his prototype; and a Don Quixote, with a bean-pole for a lance and a potlid for a shield.

But the broadest merriment was excited by a group of figures ridiculously dressed in old regimentals, which seemed to have been purchased at a military rag fair, or pilfered from some receptacle of the cast-off clothes of both the French and British armies. Portions of their attire had probably been worn at the siege of Louisburg, and the coats of most recent cut might have been rent and tattered by sword, ball, or bayonet, as long ago as Wolfe's victory. One of these worthies — a tall, lank figure, brandishing a rusty sword of immense longitude — purporting to be no less a personage than General George Washington ; and the other principal officers of the American army, such as Gates, Lee, Putnam, Schuyler, Ward, and Heath, were repre- sented by similar scarecrows. An interview in the mock-heroic style, between the rebel warriors and the British commander-in- chief, was received with immense applause, which came loudest of all from the loyalists of the colony. There was one of the guests, however, who stood apart, eying these antics sternly and scornfully, at once with a frown and a bitter smile.

It was an old man, formerly of high station and great repute in the province, and who had been a very famous soldier in his day. Some surprise had been expressed, that a person of Colonel Joliffe's known Whig principles, though now too old to take an active part in the contest, should have remained in Boston during the siege, and especially that he should consent to show himself in the mansion of Sir William Howe. But thither he had come, with a fair granddaughter under his arm ; and there, amid all the mirth and buffoonery, stood this stern old figure, the best sustained character in the masquerade, because so well representing the antique spirit of his native land. The other guests affirmed that Colonel Joliffe's black puritanical scowl threw a shadow round about him; although, in spite of his sombre influence, their gayety continued to blaze higher, like (an ominous comparison) the flickering brilliancy of a lamp which has but a little while to burn. Eleven strokes, full half an hour ago, had pealed from the clock of the Old South, when a rumor was circulated among the company that some new spectacle or pageant was about to be exhibited, which

should put a fitting close to the splendid festivities of the night.

"What new jest has your Excellency in hand?" asked the Rev. Mather Byles, whose Presbyterian scruples had not kept him from the entertainment. "Trust me, sir, I have already laughed more than beseems my cloth, at your Homeric confabulation with yonder ragamuffin general of the rebels. One other such fit of merriment, and I must throw off my clerical wig and band."

"Not so, good Dr. Byles," answered Sir William Howe; "if mirth were a crime, you had never gained your doctorate in divinity. As to this new foolery, I know no more about it than yourself; perhaps not so much. Honestly now, Doctor, have you not stirred up the sober brains of some of your countrymen to enact a scene in our masquerade?"

"Perhaps," slyly remarked the granddaughter of Colonel Joliffe, whose high spirit had been stung by many taunts against

New England, — " perhaps we are to have a mask of allegorical figures. Victory, with trophies from Lexington and Bunker Hill, — Plenty, with her overflowing horn, to typify the present abundance in this good town, — and Glory, with a wreath for his Excellency's brow."

Sir William Howe smiled at words which he would have answered with one of his darkest frowns, had they been uttered by lips that wore a beard. He was spared the necessity of a retort, by a singular interruption. A sound of music was heard without the house, as if proceeding from a full band of military instruments stationed in the street, playing, not such a festal strain as was suited to the occasion, but a slow funeral march. The drums appeared to be muffled, and the trumpets poured forth a wailing breath, which at once hushed the merriment of the auditors, filling all with wonder and some with apprehension. The idea occurred to many, that either the funeral procession of some great personage had halted in front of the Province House, or that a corpse, in a velvet-covered and gorgeously decorated coffin, was about to be borne from the portal. After listening a moment, Sir William Howe called, in a stern voice, to the leader of the musicians, who had hitherto enlivened the entertainment with gay and lightsome melodies. The man was drum-major to one of the British regiments.

" Dighton," demanded the general, " what means this foolery ? Bid your band silence that dead march ; or, by my word, they shall have sufficient cause for their lugubrious strains ! Silence it, sirrah ! "

" Please your Honor," answered the drum-major, whose rubicund visage had lost all its color, " the fault is none of mine. I and my band are all here together ; and I question whether there be a man of us that could play that march with-out book. I never heard it but once before, and that was at the funeral of his late Majesty, King George the Second."

"Well, well!" said Sir William Howe, recovering his com-posure; "it is the prelude to some masquerading antic. Let it pass."

A figure now presented itself, but, among the many fantastic masks that were dispersed through the apartments, none could tell precisely from whence it came. It was a man in an old-fashioned dress of black serge, and having the aspect of a steward, or principal domestic in the household of a nobleman, or great English landholder. This figure advanced to the outer door of the mansion, and throwing both its leaves wide open, withdrew a little to one side and looked back towards the grand staircase, as if expecting some person to descend. At the same time, the music in the street sounded a loud and dole-ful summons. The eyes of Sir William Howe and his guests being directed to the staircase, there appeared, on the upper-most landing-place that was discernible from the bottom, several personages descending towards the door. The foremost was a man of stern visage, wearing a steeple-crowned hat and a skullcap beneath it; a dark cloak, and huge wrinkled boots that came half-way up his legs. Under his arm was a rolled-up banner, which seemed to be the banner of England, but strangely rent and torn; he had a sword in his right hand, and grasped a Bible in his left. The next figure was of milder aspect, yet full of dignity, wearing a broad ruff, over which descended a beard, a gown of wrought velvet, and a doublet and hose of black satin. He carried a roll of manuscript in his hand. Close behind these two came a young man of very

"Please your honor."
"The fault is none of mine."

striking countenance and demeanor, with deep thought and contemplation on his brow, and perhaps a flash of enthusiasm in his eye. His garb, like that of his predecessors, was of an antique fashion, and there was a stain of blood upon his ruff. In the same group with these were three or four others, all men of dignity and evident command, and bearing themselves like personages who were accustomed to the gaze of the multitude. It was the idea of the beholders, that these figures went to join the mysterious funeral that had halted in front of the Province House; yet that supposition seemed to be contradicted by the air of triumph with which they waved their hands, as they crossed the threshold and vanished through the portal.

"In the Devil's name, what is this?" muttered Sir William Howe to a gentleman beside him; "a procession of the regicide judges of King Charles the martyr?"

"These," said Colonel Joliffe, breaking silence almost for the first time that evening, — "these, if I interpret them aright, are the Puritan governors, — the rulers of the old, original democracy of Massachusetts. Endicott, with the banner from which he had torn the symbol of subjection, and Winthrop, and Sir Henry Vane, and Dudley, Haynes, Bellingham, and Leverett."

"Why had that young man a stain of blood upon his ruff?" asked Miss Joliffe.

"Because, in after years," answered her grandfather, "he laid down the wisest head in England upon the block, for the principles of liberty."

"Will not your Excellency order out the guard?" whispered Lord Percy, who, with other British officers, had now assembled round the general. "There may be a plot under this mummery."

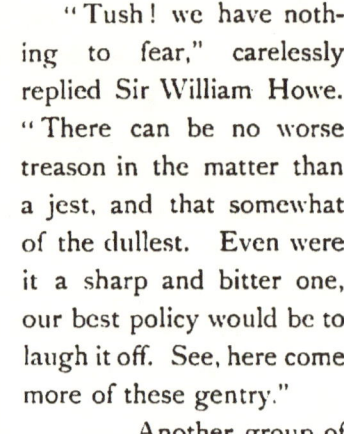

"Tush! we have nothing to fear," carelessly replied Sir William Howe. "There can be no worse treason in the matter than a jest, and that somewhat of the dullest. Even were it a sharp and bitter one, our best policy would be to laugh it off. See, here come more of these gentry."

Another group of characters had now partly descended the staircase. The first was a venerable and white-bearded patriarch, who cautiously felt his way downward with a staff. Treading hastily behind him, and stretching forth his gauntleted hand as if to grasp the old man's shoulder, came a tall, soldier-like figure, equipped with a plumed cap of steel, a bright breastplate, and a long sword, which rattled against the stairs. Next was seen a stout man, dressed in rich and courtly attire, but not of courtly demeanor; his gait had the swinging motion of a seaman's walk; and chancing to stumble on the staircase, he suddenly grew wrathful, and was heard to mutter an oath. He was followed by a noble-looking personage in a curled wig, such as are represented in the portraits of Queen Anne's time and earlier; and the breast of his coat was decorated with an embroidered star. While advancing to the door, he bowed to the right hand and to the left, in a very gracious and insinuating style; but as he crossed the threshold, unlike the early Puritan governors, he seemed to wring his hands with sorrow.

" Prithee, play the part of a chorus, good Dr. Byles," said Sir William Howe. " What worthies are these ? "

" If it please your Excellency, they lived somewhat before my day," answered the Doctor; " but doubtless our friend, the Colonel, has been hand-in-glove with them."

"Their living faces I never looked upon," said Colonel Joliffe, gravely; " although I have spoken face to face with many rulers of this land, and shall greet yet another with an old man's blessing, ere I die. But we talk of these figures. I take the venerable patriarch to be Bradstreet, the last of the Puritans, who was governor at ninety, or thereabouts. The next is Sir Edmund Andros, a tyrant, as any New England schoolboy will tell you; and therefore the people cast him down from his high seat into a dungeon. Then comes Sir William Phipps, shepherd, cooper, sea-captain, and governor: may many of his countrymen rise as high, from as low an origin! Lastly, you saw the gracious Earl of Bellamont, who ruled us under King William."

" But what is the meaning of it all ? " asked Lord Percy.

" Now, were I a rebel," said Miss Joliffe, half aloud, " I might fancy that the ghosts of these ancient governors had been summoned to form the funeral procession of royal authority in New England."

Several other figures were now seen at the turn of the staircase. The one in advance had a thoughtful, anxious, and somewhat crafty expression of face; and in spite of his loftiness of manner, which was evidently the result both of an ambitious spirit and of long continuance in high stations, he seemed not incapable of cringing to a greater than himself. A few steps behind came an officer in a scarlet and embroidered uniform, cut in a fashion old enough to have been worn by the Duke of Marlborough. His nose had a rubicund tinge, which, together with the twinkle of his eye, might have marked him as a lover of the wine-cup and good-fellowship; notwithstanding which tokens, he appeared ill at ease, and often glanced around him, as if apprehensive of some secret mischief. Next came a portly gentleman, wearing a coat of shaggy cloth, lined with silken velvet; he had sense, shrewdness, and humor in his face, and a folio volume under his arm; but his aspect was that of a man vexed and tormented beyond all patience and harassed almost to death. He went hastily down, and was followed by a dignified person, dressed in a purple velvet suit, with very rich embroidery; his demeanor would have possessed much stateliness, only that a grievous fit of the gout compelled him to hobble from stair to stair, with contortions of face and body. When Dr. Byles beheld this figure on the staircase, he shivered as with an ague, but continued to watch him steadfastly, until the gouty gentleman had reached the threshold, made a gesture of anguish and despair, and vanished into the outer gloom, whither the funeral music summoned him.

"Governor Belcher! — my old patron! — in his very shape and dress!" gasped Dr. Byles. "This is an awful mockery!"

"A tedious foolery, rather," said Sir William Howe, with an

air of indifference. "But who were the three that preceded him?"

"Governor Dudley, a cunning politician, — yet his craft once brought him to a prison," replied Colonel Joliffe; "Governor Shute, formerly a colonel under Marlborough, and whom the people frightened out of the province; and learned Governor Burnet, whom the Legislature tormented into a mortal fever."

"Methinks they were miserable men, these royal governors of Massachusetts," observed Miss Joliffe. "Heavens, how dim the light grows!"

It was certainly a fact that the large lamp which illuminated the staircase now burned dim and dusky: so that several figures, which passed hastily down the stairs and went forth from the porch, appeared rather like shadows than persons of fleshly substance. Sir William Howe and his guests stood at the doors of the contiguous apartments, watching the progress of this singular pageant, with various emotions of anger, contempt, or half-acknowledged fear, but still with an anxious curiosity. The shapes, which now seemed hastening to join the mysterious procession, were recognized rather by striking peculiarities of dress, or broad characteristics of manner, than by any perceptible resemblance of features to their prototypes. Their faces, indeed, were invariably kept in deep shadow. But Dr. Byles, and other gentlemen who had long been familiar with the successive rulers of the province, were heard to whisper the names of Shirley, of Pownall, of Sir Francis Bernard, and of the well-remembered Hutchinson; thereby confessing that the actors, whoever they might be, in this spectral march of governors, had succeeded in putting on some distant portraiture of the real personages. As they vanished from the door, still did these shadows toss their arms into the gloom of night, with a dread ex-

The Shape of Gage, as true as in a looking-glass.

pression of woe. Following the mimic representative of Hutchinson came a military figure, holding before his face the cocked hat which he had taken from his powdered head; but his epaulets and other insignia of rank were those of a general officer; and something in his mien reminded the beholders of one who had recently been master of the Province House, and chief of all the land.

"The shape of Gage, as true as in a looking-glass!" exclaimed Lord Percy, turning pale.

"No, surely," cried Miss Joliffe, laughing hysterically; "it could not be Gage, or Sir William would have greeted his old comrade in arms! Perhaps he will not suffer the next to pass unchallenged."

"Of that be assured, young lady," answered Sir William Howe, fixing his eyes, with a very marked expression, upon the immovable visage of her grandfather. "I have long enough delayed to pay the ceremonies of a host to these departing guests. The next that takes his leave shall receive due courtesy."

A wild and dreary burst of music came through the open door. It seemed as if the procession, which had been gradually filling up its ranks, were now about to move, and that this loud peal of the wailing trumpets, and roll of the muffled drums, were a call to some loiterer to make haste. Many eyes, by an irresistible impulse, were turned upon Sir William Howe, as if it were he whom the dreary music summoned to the funeral of departed power.

" See ! — here comes the last !" whispered Miss Joliffe, pointing her tremulous finger to the staircase.

A figure had come into view as if descending the stairs ; although so dusky was the region whence it emerged, some of the spectators fancied that they had seen this human shape suddenly moulding itself amid the gloom. Downward the figure came, with a stately and martial tread, and reaching the lowest stair was observed to be a tall man, booted and

wrapped in a military cloak, which was drawn up around the face
so as to meet the flapped brim of a laced hat. The features, therefore, were completely hidden. But the British officers deemed
that they had seen that military cloak before, and even recognized
the frayed embroidery on the collar, as well as the gilded scab-
bard of a sword which protruded from the folds of the cloak,
and glittered in a vivid gleam of light. Apart from these trifling
particulars, there were characteristics of gait and bearing which
impelled the wondering guests to glance from the shrouded
figure to Sir William Howe, as if to satisfy themselves that their
host had not suddenly vanished from the midst of them.

With a dark flush of wrath upon his brow, they saw the
general draw his sword and advance to meet the figure in the
cloak before the latter had stepped one pace upon the floor.

"Villain, unmuffle yourself!" cried he. "You pass no
farther!"

The figure, without blenching a hair's-breadth from the sword
which was pointed at his breast, made a solemn pause and
lowered the cape of the cloak from about his face, yet not
sufficiently for the spectators to catch a glimpse at it. But Sir
William Howe had evidently seen enough. The sternness of
his countenance gave place to a look of wild amazement, if not
horror, while he recoiled several steps from the figure, and let
fall his sword upon the floor. The martial shape again drew
the cloak about his features and passed on; but reaching the
threshold, with his back towards the spectators, he was seen to
stamp his foot and shake his clinched hands in the air. It was
afterwards affirmed that Sir William Howe had repeated that
self-same gesture of rage and sorrow, when, for the last time,
and as the last royal governor, he passed through the portal of
the Province House.

" Hark ! — the procession moves," said Miss Joliffe.

The music was dying away along the street, and its dismal strains were mingled with the knell of midnight from the steeple of the Old South, and with the roar of artillery, which announced that the beleaguering army of Washington had intrenched itself upon a nearer height than before. As the deep boom of the cannon smote upon his ear, Colonel Joliffe raised himself to the full height of his aged form, and smiled sternly on the British general.

" Would your Excellency inquire further into the mystery of the pageant ? " said he.

" Take care of your gray head ! " cried Sir William Howe, fiercely, though with a quivering lip. " It has stood too long on a traitor's shoulders ! "

" You must make haste to chop it off, then," calmly replied the Colonel ; " for a few hours longer, and not all the power of Sir William Howe, nor of his master, shall cause one of these gray hairs to fall. The empire of Britain, in this ancient province, is at its last gasp to-night ; almost while I speak it is a dead corpse ; and methinks the shadows of the old governors are fit mourners at its funeral ! "

With these words Colonel Joliffe threw on his cloak, and, drawing his granddaughter's arm within his own, retired from the last festival that a British ruler ever held in the old province of Massachusetts Bay. It was supposed that the Colonel and the young lady possessed some secret intelligence in regard to the mysterious pageant of that night. However this might be, such knowledge has never become general. The actors in the scene have vanished into deeper obscurity than even that wild Indian band who scattered the cargoes of the tea-ships on the waves, and gained a place in history, yet left no names.   But superstition, among other legends of this mansion, repeats the wondrous tale, that on the anniversary night of Britain's discomfiture, the ghosts of the ancient governors of Massachusetts still glide through the portal of the Province House. And last of all comes a figure shrouded in a military cloak, tossing his clinched hands into the air, and stamping his ironshod boots upon the broad freestone steps with a semblance of feverish despair, but without the sound of a foot-tramp. .

When the truth-telling accents of the elderly gentleman were hushed, I drew a long breath and looked round the room, striving, with the best energy of my imagination, to throw a tinge of romance and historic grandeur over the realities of the scene.   But my nostrils snuffed up a scent of cigar-smoke, clouds of which the narrator had emitted by way of visible emblem, I suppose, of the nebulous obscurity of his tale. Moreover, my gorgeous fantasies were wofully disturbed by the rattling of the spoon in a tumbler of whiskey punch, which Mr. Thomas Waite was mingling for a customer.   Nor did it add to the ·picturesque appearance of the panelled walls, that the slate of the Brookline stage was suspended against them, instead of the armorial escutcheon of some far-descended governor.   A stage-driver sat at one of the windows, reading a penny paper of the day, — the " Boston Times," — and presenting a figure which could nowise be brought into any picture of " Times in Boston," seventy or a hundred years ago.   On the window-seat lay a bundle, neatly done up in brown paper, the direction of which I had the idle curiosity to read.   " Miss SUSAN HUGGINS, at the PROVINCE HOUSE."   A pretty chambermaid, no doubt. In truth, it is desperately hard work, when we attempt to throw the spell of hoar antiquity over localities with which the living world, and the day that is passing over us, have aught to do. Yet, as I glanced at the stately staircase, down

A ftage driver
at at one of the windows reading a penny paper

which the procession of the old governors had descended, and as I emerged through the venerable portal, whence their figures had preceded me, it gladdened me to be conscious of a thrill of awe. Then diving through the narrow archway, a few strides transported me into the densest throng of Washington Street.

II.

EDWARD RANDOLPH'S PORTRAIT

THE old legendary guest of the Province House abode in my remembrance from midsummer till January. One idle evening last winter, confident that he would be found in the snuggest corner of the bar-room, I resolved to pay him another visit, hoping to deserve well of my country by snatching from oblivion some else unheard-of fact of history. The night was chill and raw, and rendered boisterous by almost a gale of wind, which whistled along Washington Street, causing the gas-lights to flare and flicker within the lamps. As I hurried onward, my fancy was busy with a comparison between the present aspect of the street, and that which it probably wore when the British governors inhabited the mansion whither I was now going. Brick edifices in those times were few, till a succession of destructive fires had swept, and swept again, the wooden dwellings and warehouses from the most populous quarters of the town. The buildings stood insulated and independent, not, as now, merging their separate existences into connected ranges, with a front of tiresome identity, but each possessing features of its own, as if the owner's individual taste had shaped it, and the whole presenting a picturesque irregularity, the absence of which is hardly compensated by any beauties of our modern architecture. Such a scene, dimly vanishing from the eye by the ray of here and there a tallow

31

candle, glimmering through the small panes of scattered windows, would form a sombre contrast to the street as I beheld it, with the gaslights blazing from corner to corner, flaming within the shops, and throwing a noonday brightness through the huge plates of glass.

But the black, lowering sky, as I turned my eyes upward, wore, doubtless, the same visage as when it frowned upon the ante-Revolutionary New-Englanders. The wintry blast had the same shriek that was familiar to their ears. The Old South Church, too, still pointed its antique spire into the darkness, and was lost between earth and heaven ; and, as I passed, its clock, which had warned so many generations how transitory was their lifetime, spoke heavily and slow the same unregarded moral to myself. "Only seven o'clock," thought I. "My old friend's legends will scarcely kill the hours 'twixt this and bedtime."

Passing through the narrow arch, I crossed the courtyard, the confined precincts of which were made visible by a lantern over the portal of the Province House. On entering the barroom, I found, as I expected, the old tradition-monger seated by a special good fire of anthracite, compelling clouds of smoke from a corpulent cigar. He recognized me with evident pleasure ; for my rare properties as a patient listener invariably made me a favorite with elderly gentlemen and ladies of narrative propensities. Drawing a chair to the fire, I desired mine host to favor us with a glass apiece of whiskey punch, which was speedily prepared, steaming hot, with a slice of lemon at the bottom, a dark red stratum of port wine upon the surface, and a sprinkling of nutmeg strewn over all. As we touched our glasses together, my legendary friend made himself known to me as Mr. Bela Tiffany; and I rejoiced at the oddity of the name, because it gave his image and character a sort of individuality in my conception. The old gentleman's draught acted as a solvent upon his memory, so that it overflowed with tales, traditions, anecdotes of famous dead people, and traits of ancient manners, some of which were childish as a nurse's lullaby, while others might have been worth the notice of the grave historian. Nothing impressed me more than a story of a black mysterious picture, which used to hang in one of the chambers of the Province House, directly above the room where we were now sitting. The following is as correct a version of the fact as the reader would be likely to obtain from any other source, although, assuredly, it has a tinge of romance approaching to the marvellous.

In one of the apartments of the Province House there was long preserved an ancient picture, the frame of which was as black as ebony, and the canvas itself so dark with age, damp, and smoke, that not a touch of the painter's art could be discerned. Time had thrown an impenetrable veil over it, and left to tradition and fable and conjecture to say what had once been there portrayed. During the rule of many successive governors it had hung, by prescriptive and undisputed right, over the mantel-piece of the same chamber; and it still kept its place when Lieutenant-Governor Hutchinson assumed the administration of the province, on the departure of Sir Francis Bernard.

The Lieutenant-Governor sat, one afternoon, resting his head against the carved back of his stately armchair, and gazing up thoughtfully at the void blackness of the picture. It was scarcely a time for such inactive musing, when affairs of the deepest moment required the ruler's decision ; for, within that very hour, Hutchinson had received intelligence of the arrival of a British fleet, bringing three regiments from Halifax to overawe the insubordination of the people. These troops awaited his per- mission to occupy the fortress of Castle William and the town itself. Yet, instead of affixing his signature to an official order, there sat the Lieutenant-Governor, so carefully scrutinizing the black waste of canvas that his demeanor attracted the notice of two young persons who attended him. One, wearing a military dress of buff, was his kinsman, Francis Lincoln, the Provincial Captain of Castle William ; the other, who sat on a low stool beside his chair, was Alice Vane, his favorite niece.

She was clad entirely in white, a pale, ethereal creature, who, though a native of New England, had been educated abroad, and seemed not merely a stranger from another clime, but almost a being from another world. For several years, until left an orphan, she had dwelt with her father in sunny Italy, and there had acquired a taste and enthusiasm for sculpture and painting, which she found few opportunities of gratifying in the undeco- rated dwellings of the colonial gentry. It was said that the early productions of her own pencil exhibited no inferior genius, though, perhaps, the rude atmosphere of New England had cramped her hand and dimmed the glowing colors of her fancy. But, observing her uncle's steadfast gaze, which appeared to search through the mist of years to discover the subject of the picture, her curiosity was excited.

" Is it known, my dear uncle," inquired she, " what this old picture once represented ? Possibly, could it be made visible, it might prove a masterpiece of some great artist ; else, why has it so long held such a conspicuous place ? "

ỹ yovng captaine of ỹ castle tells ỹ story of ỹ picture.

As her uncle, contrary to his usual custom (for he was as attentive to all the humors and caprices of Alice as if she had been his own best-beloved child), did not immediately reply, the young captain of Castle William took that office upon himself.

"This dark old square of canvas, my fair cousin," said he, "has been an heirloom in the Province House from time immemorial. As to the painter, I can tell you nothing; but, if half the stories told of it be true, not one of the great Italian masters has ever produced so marvéllous a piece of work as that before you."

Captain Lincoln proceeded to relate some of the strange fables and fantasies, which, as it was impossible to refute them by ocular demonstration, had grown to be articles of popular belief, in reference to this old picture. One of the wildest and at the same time the best accredited accounts stated it to be an original and authentic portrait of the Evil One, taken at a witch meeting near Salem; and that its strong and terrible resemblance had been confirmed by several of the confessing wizards and witches, at their trial, in open court. It was likewise affirmed that a familiar spirit, or demon, abode behind the blackness of the picture, and had shown himself, at seasons of public calamity, to more than one of the royal governors. Shirley, for instance, had beheld this ominous apparition, on the eve of General Abercrombie's shameful and bloody defeat under the walls of Ticonderoga. Many of the servants of the Province House had caught glimpses of a visage frowning down upon them, at morning or evening twilight, or in the depths of night, while raking up the fire that glimmered on the hearth beneath; although, if any were bold enough to hold a torch before the picture, it would appear as black and undistinguishable as ever. The oldest inhabitant of Boston recollected that his father, in whose days the portrait had not wholly faded out of sight, had once looked upon it, but would never suffer himself to be questioned as to the face which was there represented. In connection with such stories, it was remarkable that over the top of the frame there were some ragged remnants of black silk, indicating that a veil had formerly hung down before the picture, until the duskiness of time had so effectually concealed it. But, after all, it was the most singular part of the affair that so many of the pompous governors of Massachusetts had allowed the obliterated picture to remain in the state chamber of the Province House.

" Some of these fables are really awful," observed Alice Vane, who had occasionally shuddered, as well as smiled, while her cousin spoke. " It wou'd be almost worth while to wipe away the black surface of the canvas, since the original picture can hardly be so formidable as those which fancy paints instead of it."

" But would it be possible," inquired her cousin, " to restore this dark picture to its pristine hues ? "

" Such arts are known in Italy," said Alice.

The Lieutenant-Governor had roused himself from his abstracted mood, and listened with a smile to the conversation of his young relatives. Yet his voice had something peculiar in its tones, when he undertook the explanation of the mystery.

" I am sorry, Alice, to destroy your faith in the legends of which you are so fond," remarked he ; "but my antiquarian researches have long since made me acquainted with the subject of this picture, — if picture it can be called, — which is no more visible, nor ever will be, than the face of the long-buried man whom it once represented. It was the portrait of Edward

Randolph, the founder of this house, a person famous in the history of New England."

"Of that Edward Randolph," exclaimed Captain Lincoln, "who obtained the repeal of the first provincial charter, under which our forefathers had enjoyed almost democratic privileges! He that was styled the arch-enemy of New England, and whose memory is still held in detestation, as the destroyer of our liberties!"

"It was the same Randolph," answered Hutchinson, moving uneasily in his chair. "It was his lot to taste the bitterness of popular odium."

"Our annals tell us," continued the Captain of Castle William, "that the curse of the people followed this Randolph where he went, and wrought evil in all the subsequent events of his life, and that its effect was seen likewise in the manner of his death. They say, too, that the inward misery of that curse worked itself outward, and was visible on the wretched man's countenance, making it too horrible to be looked upon. If so, and if this picture truly represented his aspect, it was in mercy that the cloud of blackness has gathered over it."

"These traditions are folly to one who has proved, as I have, how little of historic truth lies at the bottom," said the Lieutenant-Governor. "As regards the life and character of Edward Randolph, too implicit credence has been given to Dr. Cotton Mather, who — I must say it, though some of his blood runs in my veins — has filled our early history with old women's tales, as fanciful and extravagant as those of Greece or Rome."

"And yet," whispered Alice Vane, "may not such fables have a moral? And, methinks, if the visage of this portrait be so dreadful, it is not without a cause that it has hung so long in

a chamber of the Province House. When the rulers feel themselves irresponsible, it were well that they should be reminded
of the awful weight of a people's curse."

The Lieutenant-Governor started, and gazed for a moment
at his niece, as if her girlish fantasies had struck upon some
feeling in his own breast, which all his policy or principles could
not entirely subdue. He knew, indeed, that Alice, in spite of
her foreign education, retained the native sympathies of a New
England girl.

"Peace, silly child," cried he, at last, more harshly than he
had ever before addressed the gentle Alice. "The rebuke of a
king is more to be dreaded than the clamor of a wild, misguided
multitude. Captain Lincoln, it is decided. The fortress of
Castle William must be occupied by the royal troops. The
two remaining regiments shall be billeted in the town, or
encamped upon the Common. It is time, after years of tumult,
and almost rebellion, that his Majesty's government should have
a wall of strength about it."

"Trust, sir, — trust yet awhile to the loyalty of the people,"
said Captain Lincoln ; "nor teach them that they can ever be
on other terms with British soldiers than those of brotherhood,
as when they fought side by side through the French war. Do
not convert the streets of your native town into a camp. Think
twice before you give up old Castle William, the key of the
province, into other keeping than that of true-born New-
Englanders."

"Young man, it is decided," repeated Hutchinson, rising from
his chair. "A British officer will be in attendance this evening
to receive the necessary instructions for the disposal of the troops.
Your presence also will be required. Till then, farewell."

With these words the Lieutenant-Governor hastily left the room, while Alice and her cousin more slowly followed, whispering together, and once pausing to glance back at the mysterious picture. The Captain of Castle William fancied that the girl's air and mien were such as might have belonged to one of those spirits of fable — fairies, or creatures of a more antique mythology — who sometimes mingled their agency with mortal affairs, half in caprice, yet with a sensibility to human weal or woe. As he held the door for her to pass, Alice beckoned to the picture and smiled.

Alice beckoned to the picture

"Come forth, dark and evil shape!" cried she. "It is thine hour!"

In the evening, Lieutenant-Governor Hutchinson sat in the same chamber where the foregoing scene had occurred, surrounded by several persons whose various interests had summoned them together. There were the Selectmen of Boston, plain, patriarchal fathers of the people, excellent representatives of the old puritanical founders, whose sombre strength had stamped so deep an impress upon the New England character. Contrasting with these were one or two members of Council, richly dressed in the white wigs, the embroidered waistcoats, and other magnificence of the time, and making a somewhat ostentatious display of courtier-like ceremonial. In attendance, likewise, was a major of the British army, awaiting the Lieutenant-Governor's orders for the landing of the troops, which still remained on board the transports. The Captain of Castle William stood beside Hutchinson's chair, with folded arms, glancing rather haughtily at the British officer, by whom he was soon to be superseded in his command. On a table, in the centre of the chamber, stood a branched silver candlestick, throwing down the glow of half a dozen wax lights upon a paper, apparently ready for the Lieutenant-Governor's signature.

Partly shrouded in the voluminous folds of one of the window-curtains, which fell from the ceiling to the floor, was seen the white drapery of a lady's robe. It may appear strange that Alice Vane should have been there, at such a time; but there was something so childlike, so wayward, in her singular character, so apart from ordinary rules, that her presence did not surprise the few who noticed it. Meantime, the chairman of the Selectmen was addressing to the Lieutenant-Governor a long and solemn protest against the reception of the British troops into the town.

" And if your Honor," concluded this excellent but somewhat prosy gentleman, " shall see fit to persist in bringing these mercenary sworders and musketeers into our quiet streets, not on our heads be the responsibility. Think, sir, while there is yet time, that if one drop of blood be shed, that blood shall be an eternal stain upon your Honor's memory. You, sir, have written, with an able pen, the deeds of our forefathers. The more to be desired is it, therefore, that yourself should deserve

honorable mention, as a true patriot and upright ruler, when your own doings shall be written down in history."

" I am not-insensible, my good sir, to the natural desire to stand well in the annals of my country," replied Hutchinson, controlling his impatience into courtesy, " nor know I any better method of attaining that end than by withstanding the merely temporary spirit of mischief, which, with your pardon, seems to have infected elder men than myself. Would you have me wait till the mob shall sack the Province House, as they did my private mansion? Trust me, sir, the time may come when you will be glad to flee for protection to the king's banner, the raising of which is now so distasteful to you."

" Yes," said the British major, who was impatiently expecting the Lieutenant-Governor's orders. " The demagogues of this province have raised the devil, and cannot lay him again. We will exorcise him, in God's name and the king's."

" If you meddle with the devil, take care of his claws!" answered the Captain of Castle William, stirred by the taunt against his countrymen.

" Craving your pardon, young sir," said the venerable Selectman, " let not an evil spirit enter into your words. We will strive against the oppressor with prayer and fasting, as our forefathers would have done. Like them, moreover, we will submit to whatever lot a wise Providence may send us, — always, after our own best exertions to amend it."

" And there peep forth the devil's claws!" muttered Hutchinson, who well understood the nature of Puritan submission. "This matter shall be expedited forthwith. When there shall be a sentinel at every corner, and a court of guard before the town-house, a loyal gentleman may venture to walk abroad.

What to me is the outcry of a mob, in this remote province of the realm? The King is my master, and England is my country! Upheld by their armed strength, I set my foot upon the rabble, and defy them!"

He snatched a pen, and was about to affix his signature to the paper that lay on the table, when the Captain of Castle William placed his hand upon his shoulder. The freedom of the action, so contrary to the ceremonious respect which was then considered due to rank and dignity, awakened general surprise, and in none more than in the Lieutenant-Governor himself. Looking angrily up, he perceived that his young relative was pointing his finger to the opposite wall. Hutchinson's eye followed the signal; and he saw, what had hitherto been unobserved, that a black silk curtain was suspended before the mysterious picture, so as completely to conceal it. His thoughts immediately recurred to the scene of the preceding afternoon; and, in his surprise, confused by indistinct emotions, yet sensible that his niece must have had an agency in this phenomenon, he called loudly upon her.

"Alice! — come hither, Alice!"

No sooner had he spoken than Alice Vane glided from her station, and, pressing one hand across her eyes, with the other snatched away the sable curtain that concealed the portrait. An exclamation of surprise burst from every beholder; but the Lieutenant-Governor's voice had a tone of horror.

"By Heaven," said he, in a low, inward murmur, speaking rather to himself than to those around him, "if the spirit of Edward Randolph were to appear among us from the place of torment, he could not wear more of the terrors of hell upon his face!"

" For some wise end," said the aged Selectman solemnly, " hath Providence scattered away the mist of years that had so long hid this dreadful effigy. Until this hour no living man hath seen what we behold ! "

Within the antique frame, which so recently had enclosed a sable waste of canvas, now appeared a visible picture, still dark, indeed, in its hues and shadings, but thrown forward in strong relief. It was a half-length figure of a gentleman in a rich but very old-fashioned dress of embroidered velvet, with a broad ruff and a beard, and wearing a hat, the brim of which over-

She stretched away the sable curtain.

shadowed his forehead. Beneath this cloud the eyes had a peculiar glare which was almost life-like. The whole portrait started so distinctly out of the background that it had the effect of a person looking down from the wall at the astonished and awe-stricken spectators. The expression of the face, if any words can convey an idea of it, was that of a wretch detected in some hideous guilt, and exposed to the bitter hatred and laughter and withering scorn of a vast surrounding multitude. There was the struggle of defiance, beaten down and overwhelmed by the crushing weight of ignominy. The torture of the soul had come forth upon the countenance. It seemed as if the picture, while hidden behind the cloud of immemorial years, had been all the time acquiring an intenser depth and darkness of expression, till now it gloomed forth again, and threw its evil omen over the present hour. Such, if the wild legend may be credited, was the portrait of Edward Randolph, as he appeared when a people's curse had wrought its influence upon his nature.

"'Twould drive me mad, — that awful face!" said Hutchinson, who seemed fascinated by the contemplation of it.

"Be warned, then!" whispered Alice. "He trampled on a people's rights. Behold his punishment, — and avoid a crime like his!"

The Lieutenant-Governor actually trembled for an instant; but, exerting his energy, — which was not, however, his most characteristic feature, — he strove to shake off the spell of Randolph's countenance.

"Girl!" cried he, laughing bitterly, as he turned to Alice, "have you brought hither your painter's art, — your Italian spirit of intrigue, — your tricks of stage effect, — and think to influence the councils of rulers and the affairs of nations by such shallow contrivances? See here!"

"Stay yet awhile," said the Selectman, as Hutchinson again snatched the pen; "for if ever mortal man received a warning from a tormented soul, your Honor is that man!"

"Away!" answered Hutchinson fiercely. "Though yonder senseless picture cried, 'Forbear!' it should not move me!"

Casting a scowl of defiance at the pictured face (which seemed, at that moment, to intensify the horror of its miserable and wicked look), he scrawled on the paper, in characters that betokened it a deed of desperation, the name of Thomas

Hutchinson. Then, it is said, he shuddered, as if that signature had granted away his salvation.

" It is done," said he ; and placed his hand upon his brow.

" May Heaven forgive the deed," said the soft, sad accents of Alice Vane, like the voice of a good spirit flitting away.

When morning came there was a stifled whisper through the household, and spreading thence about the town, that the dark, mysterious picture had started from the wall, and spoken face to face with Lieutenant-Governor Hutchinson. If such a miracle had been wrought, however, no traces of it remained behind ; for within the antique frame nothing could be discerned, save the impenetrable cloud which had covered the canvas since the memory of man. If the figure had, indeed, stepped forth, it had fled back, spirit-like, at the day-dawn, and hidden itself behind a century's obscurity. The truth probably was that Alice Vane's secret for restoring the hues of the picture had merely effected a temporary renovation. But those who, in that brief interval, had beheld the awful visage of Edward Randolph, desired no second glance, and ever afterwards trembled at the recollection of the scene, as if an evil spirit had appeared visibly among them. And as for Hutchinson, when, far over the ocean, his dying hour drew on, he gasped for breath, and complained that he was choking with the blood of the Boston massacre ; and Francis Lincoln, the former Captain of Castle William, who was standing at his bed-side, perceived a likeness in his frenzied look to that of Edward Randolph. Did his broken spirit feel, at that dread hour, the tremendous burden of a people's curse ?

At the conclusion of this miraculous legend, I inquired of mine host whether the picture still remained in the chamber over our heads ; but Mr. Tiffany informed me that it had long since been removed, and was supposed to be hidden in some out-of-the-way corner of the New England Museum. Perchance some curious antiquary may light upon it there, and, with the assistance of Mr. Howorth, the picture-cleaner, may supply a not unnecessary proof of the authenticity of the facts here set down. During the progress of the story a storm had been gathering abroad, and raging and rattling so loudly in the upper regions of the Province House, that it seemed as if all the old governors and great men were running riot above stairs, while Mr. Bela Tiffany babbled of them below. In the course of generations, when many people have lived and died in an ancient house, the whistling of the wind through its crannies, and the creaking of its beams and rafters, become strangely like the tones of the human voice, or thundering laughter, or heavy footsteps treading the deserted chambers. It is as if the echoes of half a century were revived. Such were the ghostly sounds that roared and murmured in our ears, when I took leave of the circle round the fireside of the Province House, and, plunging down the doorsteps, fought my way homeward against a drifting snow-storm.

III.

LADY ELEANORE'S MANTLE.

MINE excellent friend, the landlord of the Province House, was pleased, the other evening, to invite Mr. Tiffany and myself to an oyster-supper. This slight mark of respect and gratitude, as he handsomely observed, was far less than the ingenious tale-teller, and I, the humble note-taker of his narratives, had fairly earned, by the public notice which our joint lucubrations had attracted to his establishment. Many a cigar had been smoked within his premises, — many a glass of wine, or more potent aqua vitæ, had been quaffed, — many a dinner had been eaten by curious strangers, who, save for the fortunate conjunction of Mr. Tiffany and me, would never have ventured through that darksome avenue which gives access to the historic precincts of the Province House. In short, if any credit be due to the courteous assurances of Mr. Thomas Waite, we had brought his forgotten mansion almost as effectually into public view as if we had thrown down the vulgar range of shoe-shops and dry-goods stores which hides its aristocratic front from Washington Street. It may be unadvisable, however, to speak too loudly of the increased custom of the house, lest Mr. Waite should find it difficult to renew the lease on so favorable terms as heretofore.

Being thus welcomed as benefactors, neither Mr. Tiffany nor myself felt any scruple in doing full justice to the good things that were set before us. If the feast were less magnificent than

those same panelled walls had witnessed in a bygone century,
— if mine host presided with somewhat less of state than might
have befitted a successor of the royal governors, — if the
guests made a less imposing show than the bewigged and powdered and embroidered dignitaries who erst banqueted at the
gubernatorial table, and now sleep within their armorial tombs
on Copp's Hill or round King's Chapel, — yet never, I may
boldly say, did a more comfortable little party assemble in the
Province House, from Queen Anne's days to the Revolution.
The occasion was rendered more interesting by the presence of
a venerable personage, whose own actual reminiscences went
back to the epoch of Gage and Howe, and even supplied him
with a doubtful anecdote or two of Hutchinson.   He was one
of that small, and now all but extinguished class, whose attach-
ment to royalty, and to the colonial institutions and customs
that were connected with it, had never yielded to the democratic heresies of after times.   The young queen of Britain has
not a more loyal subject in her realm — perhaps not one who
would kneel before her throne with such reverential love — than
this old grandsire, whose head has whitened beneath the mild
sway of the Republic, which still, in his mellower moments, he
terms a usurpation.   Yet prejudices so obstinate have not made
him an ungentle or impracticable companion.   If the truth must
be told, the life of the aged loyalist has been of such a scram-
bling and unsettled character, — he has had so little choice of
friends, and been so often destitute of any, — that I doubt
whether he would refuse a cup of kindness with either Oliver
Cromwell or John Hancock; to say nothing of any democrat
now upon the stage.   In another paper of this series, I may,
perhaps, give the reader a closer glimpse of his portrait.

Our host, in due season, uncorked a bottle of Madeira of such exquisite perfume and desirable flavor that he surely must have discovered it in an ancient bin, down deep beneath the deepest cellar, where some jolly old butler stored away the Governor's choicest wine, and forgot to reveal the secret on his death-bed. Peace to his red-nosed ghost, and a libation to his memory! This precious liquor was imbibed by Mr. Tiffany with peculiar zest; and, after sipping the third glass, it was his pleasure to give us one of the oddest legends which he had yet raked from the storehouse where he keeps such matters. With some suitable adornments from my own fancy, it ran pretty much as follows.

Not long after Colonel Shute had assumed the government of Massachusetts Bay, now nearly a hundred and twenty years ago, a young lady of rank and fortune arrived from England, to claim his protection as her guardian. He was her distant relative, but the nearest who had survived the gradual extinction of her family; so that no more eligible shelter could be found for the rich and high-born Lady Eleanore Rochcliffe than within the Province House of a transatlantic colony. The consort of Governor Shute, moreover, had been as a mother to her childhood, and was now anxious to receive her, in the hope that a beautiful young woman would be exposed to infinitely less peril from the primitive society of New England than amid the artifices and corruptions of a court. If either the Governor or his lady had especially consulted their own comfort, they would probably have sought to devolve the responsibility on other hands; since, with some noble and splendid traits of character, Lady Eleanore was remarkable for a harsh, unyielding pride, a haughty consciousness of her hereditary and personal advantages, which made her almost incapable of control. Judging from many traditionary anecdotes, this peculiar temper was hardly less than a monomania; or, if the acts which it inspired were those of a sane person, it seemed due from Providence that pride so sinful should be followed by as severe a retribution. That tinge of the marvellous which is thrown over so many of these half-forgotten legends has probably imparted an additional wildness to the strange story of Lady Eleanore Rochcliffe.

The ship in which she came passenger had arrived at Newport, whence Lady Eleanore was conveyed to Boston in the Governor's coach, attended by a small escort of gentlemen on horseback. The ponderous equipage, with its four black horses, attracted much notice as it rumbled through Cornhill, surrounded by the prancing steeds of half a dozen cavaliers, with swords dangling to their stirrups and pistols at their holsters. Through the large glass windows of the coach, as it rolled along, the people could discern the figure of Lady Eleanore, strangely combining an almost queenly stateliness with the grace and beauty of a maiden in her teens. A singular tale had gone abroad among the ladies of the province, that their fair rival was indebted for much of the irresistible charm of her appearance to a certain article of dress, — an embroidered mantle, — which had been wrought by the most skilful artist in London, and possessed even magical properties of adornment. On the present occasion, however, she owed nothing to the witchery of dress, being clad in a riding-habit of velvet, which would have appeared stiff and ungraceful on any other form.

The coachman reined in his four black steeds, and the whole

𝔂 beauteous Ladye Eleanore cometh to Boston —

cavalcade came to a pause in front of the contorted iron balustrade that fenced the Province House from the public street.
It was an awkward coincidence that the bell of the Old South
was just then tolling for a funeral ; so that, instead of a gladsome
peal, with which it was customary to announce the arrival of
distinguished strangers, Lady Eleanore Rochcliffe was ushered
by a doleful clang, as if calamity had come embodied in her
beautiful person.

"A very great disrespect !" exclaimed Captain Langford, an
English officer, who had recently brought despatches to Gov-
ernor Shute. "The funeral should have been deferred, lest
Lady Eleanore's spirits be affected by such a dismal welcome."

"With your pardon, sir," replied Dr. Clarke, a physician, and
a famous champion of the popular party, "whatever the heralds
may pretend, a dead beggar must have precedence of a living
queen. King Death confers high privileges."

These remarks were interchanged while the speakers waited
a passage through the crowd, which had gathered on each side
of the gateway, leaving an open avenue to the portal of the
Province House. A black slave in livery now leaped from
behind the coach, and threw open the door ; while at the same
moment Governor Shute descended the flight of steps from his
mansion, to assist Lady Eleanore in alighting. But the Governor's stately approach was anticipated in a manner that excited
general astonishment. A pale young man, with his black hair
all in disorder, rushed from the throng, and prostrated himself
beside the coach, thus offering his person as a footstool for Lady
Eleanore Rochcliffe to tread upon. She held back an instant ;
yet with an expression as if doubting whether the young man
were worthy to bear the weight of her footstep, rather than

dissatisfied to receive such awful reverence from a fellow-mortal.

"Up, sir," said the Governor sternly, at the same time lift-ing his cane over the intruder. "What means the Bedlamite by this freak?"

Governor Shute descended the flight of steps

"Nay," answered Lady Eleanore play-fully, but with more scorn than pity in her tone, "your Excel-lency shall not strike him. When men seek only to be trampled upon, it were a pity to deny them a favor so easily granted — and so well deserved."

Then, though as lightly as a sunbeam on a cloud, she placed her foot upon the cowering form, and extended her hand to meet that of the Governor. There was a brief interval, during which Lady Eleanore retained this attitude; and never, surely, was there an apter emblem of aristocracy and hereditary pride tram-pling on human sympathies and the kindred of nature than these two figures presented at that moment. Yet the spectators

were so smitten with her beauty, and so essential did pride seem
to the existence of such a creature, that they gave a simultaneous
acclamation of applause.

"Who is this insolent young fellow?" inquired Captain
Langford, who still remained beside Dr. Clarke. "If he be
in his senses, his impertinence demands the bastinado. If mad,
Lady Eleanore should be secured from further inconvenience, by
his confinement."

"His name is Jervase Helwyse," answered the Doctor; "a
youth of no birth or fortune, or other advantages, save the mind
and soul that nature gave him; and, being secretary to our colonial agent in London, it was his misfortune to meet this Lady
Eleanore Rochcliffe. He loved her, — and her scorn has driven
him mad."

"He was mad so to aspire," observed the English officer.

"It may be so," said Dr. Clarke, frowning as he spoke.
"But I tell you, sir, I could well-nigh doubt the justice of the
heaven above us, if no signal humiliation overtake this lady,
who now treads so haughtily into yonder mansion. She seeks
to place herself above the sympathies of our common nature,
which envelops all human souls. See, if that nature do not
assert its claim over her in some mode that shall bring her level
with the lowest!"

"Never!" cried Captain Langford indignantly; "neither in
life, nor when they lay her with her ancestors."

Not many days afterwards the Governor gave a ball in honor
of Lady Eleanore Rochcliffe. The principal gentry of the colony
received invitations, which were distributed to their residences,
far and near, by messengers on horseback, bearing missives
sealed with all the formality of official despatches. In obedience

to the summons, there was a general gathering of rank, wealth, and beauty; and the wide door of the Province House had seldom given admittance to more numerous and honorable guests than on the evening of Lady Eleanore's ball. Without much extravagance of eulogy, the spectacle might even be termed splendid; for, according to the fashion of the times, the ladies shone in rich silks and satins, outspread over wide-projecting hoops; and the gentlemen glittered in gold embroidery, laid unsparingly upon the purple, or scarlet, or sky-blue velvet, which was the material of their coats and waistcoats. The latter article of dress was of great importance, since it enveloped the wearer's body nearly to the knees, and was perhaps bedizened with the amount of his whole year's income, in golden flowers and foliage. The altered taste of the present day — a taste symbolic of a deep change in the whole system of society — would look upon almost any of those gorgeous figures as ridiculous; although that evening the guests sought their reflections in the pier-glasses, and rejoiced to catch their own glitter amid the glittering crowd. What a pity that one of the stately mirrors has not preserved a picture of the scene, which, by the very traits that were so transitory, might have taught us much that would be worth knowing and remembering.

Would, at least, that either painter or mirror could convey to us some faint idea of a garment, already noticed in this legend, — the Lady Eleanore's embroidered mantle, — which the gossips whispered was invested with magic properties, so as to lend a new and untried grace to her figure each time that she put it on! Idle fancy as it is, this mysterious mantle has thrown an awe around my image of her, partly from its fabled virtues, and partly because it was the handiwork of a dying

A gathering of rank, wealth and beauty

woman, and, perchance, owed the fantastic grace of its conception to the delirium of approaching death.

After the ceremonial greetings had been paid, Lady Eleanore Rochcliffe stood apart from the mob of guests, insulating herself within a small and distinguished circle, to whom she accorded a more cordial favor than to the general throng. The waxen torches threw their radiance vividly over the scene, bringing out its brilliant points in strong relief; but she gazed carelessly, and with now and then an expression of weariness or scorn, tempered with such feminine grace that her auditors scarcely perceived the moral deformity of which it was the utterance. She beheld the spectacle, not with vulgar ridicule, as disdaining to be pleased with the provincial mockery of a court festival, but with the deeper scorn of one whose spirit held itself too high to participate in the enjoyment of other human souls. Whether or no the recollections of those who saw her that evening were influenced by the strange events with which she was subsequently connected, so it was that her figure ever after recurred to them as marked by something wild and unnatural; although, at the time, the general whisper was of her exceeding beauty, and of the indescribable charm which her mantle threw around her. Some close observers, indeed, detected a feverish flush and alternate paleness of countenance, with a corresponding flow and revulsion of spirits, and once or twice a painful and helpless betrayal of lassitude, as if she were on the point of sinking to the ground. Then, with a nervous shudder, she seemed to arouse her energies, and threw some bright and playful, yet half-wicked sarcasm into the conversation. There was so strange a characteristic in her manners and sentiments that it astonished every right-minded listener; till, looking in her face, a lurking and incomprehensible glance and smile perplexed them with doubts both as to her seriousness and sanity. Gradually, Lady Eleanore Rochcliffe's circle grew smaller, till only four gentlemen remained in it. These were Captain Langford, the English officer before mentioned; a Virginian planter, who had come to Massachusetts on some political errand; a young Episcopal clergyman, the grandson of a British Earl; and, lastly, the private secretary of Governor Shute, whose obsequiousness had won a sort of tolerance from Lady Eleanore.

At different periods of the evening the liveried servants of the Province House passed among the guests, bearing huge trays of refreshments, and French and Spanish wines. Lady Eleanore Rochcliffe, who refused to wet her beautiful lips even with a bubble of champagne, had sunk back into a large damask chair, apparently overwearied either with the excitement of the scene or its tedium; and while, for an instant, she was unconscious of voices, laughter, and music, a young man stole forward, and knelt down at her feet. He bore a salver in his hand, on which was a chased silver goblet, filled to the brim with wine, which he offered as reverentially as to a crowned queen, or rather with the awful devotion of a priest doing sacrifice to his idol. Conscious that some one touched her robe, Lady Eleanore started, and unclosed her eyes upon the pale, wild features and dishevelled hair of Jervase Helwyse.

"Why do you haunt me thus?" said she, in a languid tone, but with a kindlier feeling than she ordinarily permitted herself to express. "They tell me that I have done you harm."

"Heaven knows if that be so," replied the young man solemnly. "But, Lady Eleanore, in requital of that harm, if

"I pray you take one sip of this holy wine.

such there be, and for your own earthly and heavenly welfare, I
pray you to take one sip of this holy wine, and then to pass the
goblet round among the guests. And this shall be a symbol
that you have not sought to withdraw yourself from the chain
of human sympathies, — which whoso would shake off must
keep company with fallen angels."

"Where has this mad fellow stolen that sacramental vessel?"
exclaimed the Episcopal clergyman.

This question drew the notice of the guests to the silver cup,
which was recognized as appertaining to the communion plate
of the Old South Church ; and, for aught that could be known,
it was brimming over with the consecrated wine.

"Perhaps it is poisoned," half whispered the Governor's
secretary.

"Pour it down the villain's throat!" cried the Virginian
fiercely.

"Turn him out of the house!" cried Captain Langford,
seizing Jervase Helwyse so roughly by the shoulder that the
sacramental cup was overturned, and its contents sprinkled
upon Lady Eleanore's mantle. "Whether knave, fool, or
Bedlamite, it is intolerable that the fellow should go at large."

"Pray, gentlemen, do my poor admirer no harm," said Lady
Eleanore, with a faint and weary smile. "Take him out of my
sight, if such be your pleasure ; for I can find in my heart to do
nothing but laugh at him ; whereas, in all decency and con-
science, it would become me to weep for the mischief I have
wrought!"

But while the bystanders were attempting to lead away the
unfortunate young man, he broke from them, and, with a wild,
impassioned earnestness, offered a new and equally strange

petition to Lady Eleanore. It was no other than that she should throw off the mantle, which, while he pressed the silver cup of wine upon her, she had drawn more closely around her form, so as almost to shroud herself within it.

"Cast it from you!" exclaimed Jervase Helwyse, clasping his hands in an agony of entreaty. "It may not yet be too late! Give the accursed garment to the flames!"

But Lady Eleanore, with a laugh of scorn, drew the rich folds of the embroidered mantle over her head, in such a fashion as to give a completely new aspect to her beautiful face, which — half hidden, half revealed — seemed to belong to some being of mysterious character and purposes.

"Farewell, Jervase Helwyse!" said she. "Keep my image in your remembrance, as you behold it now."

"Alas, lady!" he replied, in a tone no longer wild, but sad as a funeral bell. "We must meet shortly, when your face may wear another aspect, and that shall be the image that must abide within me."

He made no more resistance to the violent efforts of the gentlemen and servants, who almost dragged him out of the apartment, and dismissed him roughly from the iron gate of the Province House. Captain Langford, who had been very active in this affair, was returning to the presence of Lady Eleanore Rochcliffe, when he encountered the physician, Dr. Clarke, with whom he had held some casual talk on the day of her arrival. The Doctor stood apart, separated from Lady Eleanore by the width of the room, but eying her with such keen sagacity that Captain Langford involuntarily gave him credit for the discovery of some deep secret.

"You appear to be smitten, after all, with the charms of this

Keep my image in your remembrance

queenly maiden," said he, hoping thus to draw forth the physician's hidden knowledge.

"God forbid!" answered Dr. Clarke, with a grave smile; "and if you be wise, you will put up the same prayer for yourself. Woe to those who shall be smitten by this beautiful Lady Eleanore! But yonder stands the Governor, and I have a word or two for his private ear. Good night!"

The communication could be of no agreeable import.

He accordingly advanced to Governor Shute, and addressed him in so low a tone that none of the bystanders could catch a word of what he said; although the sudden change of his Excellency's hitherto cheerful visage betokened that the communication could be of no agreeable import. A very few moments afterwards, it was announced to the guests that an unforeseen circumstance rendered it necessary to put a premature close to the festival.

The ball at the Province House supplied a topic of conversation for the colonial metropolis for some days after its occurrence, and might still longer have been the general theme, only that a subject of all-engrossing interest thrust it, for a time, from the public recollection. This was the appearance of a dreadful epidemic, which in that age, and long before and afterwards, was wont to slay its hundreds and thousands on both sides of the

Atlantic. On the occasion of which we speak, it was distinguished by a peculiar virulence, insomuch that it has left its traces — its pit-marks, to use an appropriate figure — on the history of the country, the affairs of which were thrown into confusion by its ravages. At first, unlike its ordinary course, the disease seemed to confine itself to the higher circles of society, selecting its victims from among the proud, the well-born, and the wealthy; entering unabashed into stately chambers, and lying down with the slumberers in silken beds. Some of the most distinguished guests of the Province House — even those whom the haughty Lady Eleanore Rochcliffe had deemed not unworthy of her favor — were stricken by this fatal scourge. It was noticed, with an ungenerous bitterness of feeling, that the four gentlemen — the Virginian, the British officer, the young clergyman, and the Governor's secretary — who had been her most devoted attendants on the evening of the ball, were the foremost on whom the plague-stroke fell. But the disease, pursuing its onward progress, soon ceased to be exclusively a prerogative of aristocracy. Its red brand was no longer conferred like a noble's star, or an order of knighthood. It threaded its way through the narrow and crooked streets, and entered the low, mean, darksome dwellings, and laid its hand of death upon the artisans and laboring classes of the town. It compelled rich and poor to feel themselves brethren, then; and stalking to and fro across the Three Hills, with a fierceness which made it almost a new pestilence, there was that mighty conqueror — that scourge and horror of our forefathers — the Small-Pox!

We cannot estimate the affright which this plague inspired of yore, by contemplating it as the fangless monster of the present day. We must remember, rather, with what awe we watched the gigantic footsteps of the Asiatic cholera, striding from shore to shore of the Atlantic, and marching like destiny upon cities far remote, which flight had already half depopulated. There is no other fear so horrible and unhumanizing as that which makes man dread to breathe Heaven's vital air, lest it be poison, or to grasp the hand of a brother or friend, lest the gripe of the pestilence should clutch him. Such was the dismay that now followed in the track of the disease, or ran before it throughout the town. Graves were hastily dug, and the pestilential relics as hastily covered, because the dead were enemies of the living, and strove to draw them headlong, as it were, into their own dismal pit. The public councils were suspended, as if mortal wisdom might relinquish its devices, now that an unearthly usurper had found his way into the ruler's mansion. Had an enemy's fleet been hovering on the coast, or his armies trampling on our soil, the people would probably have committed their defence to that same direful conqueror who had wrought their own calamity, and would permit no interference with his sway. This conqueror had a symbol of his triumphs. It was a blood-red flag, that fluttered in the tainted air over the door of every dwelling into which the Small-Pox had entered.

Such a banner was long since waving over the portal of the Province House; for thence, as was proved by tracking its footsteps back, had all this dreadful mischief issued. It had been traced back to a lady's luxurious chamber, — to the proudest of the proud, — to her that was so delicate, and hardly owned herself of earthly mould, — to the haughty one, who took her stand above human sympathies, — to Lady Eleanore! There remained no room for doubt that the contagion had lurked in that gorgeous mantle, which threw so strange a grace around her at the festival.   Its fantastic splendor had been conceived in the delirious brain of a woman on her death-bed, and was the last toil of her stiffening fingers, which had interwoven fate and misery with its golden threads.   This dark tale, whispered at first, was now bruited far and wide.   The people raved against the Lady Eleanore, and cried out that her pride and scorn had evoked a fiend, and that, between them both, this monstrous evil had been born.   At times, their rage and despair took the semblance of grinning mirth ; and whenever the red flag of the pestilence was hoisted over another and yet another door, they clapped their hands and shouted through the streets in bitter mockery, " Behold a new triumph for the Lady Eleanore ! "

One day, in the midst of these dismal times, a wild figure approached the portal of the Province House, and, folding his arms, stood contemplating the scarlet banner, which a passing breeze shook fitfully, as if to fling abroad the contagion that it typified.   At length, climbing one of the pillars by means of the iron balustrade, he took down the flag, and entered the mansion, waving it above his head.   At the foot of the staircase he met the Governor, booted and spurred, with his cloak drawn around him, evidently on the point of setting forth upon a journey.

"Wretched lunatic, what do you seek here ? " exclaimed Shute, extending his cane to guard himself from contact. " There is nothing here but Death.   Back, — or you will meet him ! "

" Death will not touch me, the banner-bearer of the pestilence ! " cried Jervase Helwyse, shaking the red flag aloft. " Death and the Pestilence, who wears the aspect of the Lady Eleanore, will walk through the streets to-night, and I must march before them with this banner ! "

"Why do I waste words on the fellow?" muttered the Governor, drawing his cloak across his mouth. "What matters his miserable life, when none of us are sure of twelve hours' breath? On, fool, to your own destruction!"

He made way for Jervase Helwyse, who immediately ascended the staircase, but, on the first landing-place, was arrested by the firm grasp of a hand upon his shoulder. Look-ing fiercely up, with a madman's impulse to struggle with and rend asunder his opponent, he found himself power-less beneath a calm, stern eye, which possessed the mysterious property of quelling frenzy at its height. The person whom he had now encountered was the physician, Dr. Clarke, the duties of whose sad profession had led him to the Province House, where he was an infre-quent guest in more prosperous times.

"Young man, what is your purpose?"

"Young man, what is your purpose?" demanded he.

"I seek the Lady Eleanore," answered Jervase Helwyse submissively.

"All have fled from her," said the physician. "Why do you seek her now? I tell you, youth, her nurse fell death-stricken on the threshold of that fatal chamber. Know ye not that never came such a curse to our shores as this lovely Lady Eleanore?—that her breath has filled the air with poison?—that she has shaken pestilence and death upon the land, from the folds of her accursed mantle?"

"Let me look upon her!" rejoined the mad youth more wildly. "Let me behold her, in her awful beauty, clad in the regal garments of the pestilence! She and Death sit on a throne together. Let me kneel down before them!"

"Poor youth!" said Dr. Clarke; and, moved by a deep sense of human weakness, a smile of caustic humor curled his lip even then. "Wilt thou still worship the destroyer, and surround her image with fantasies the more magnificent, the more evil she has wrought? Thus man doth ever to his tyrants! Approach, then! Madness, as I have noted, has that good efficacy that it will guard you from contagion; and perchance its own cure may be found in yonder chamber."

Ascending another flight of stairs, he threw open a door, and signed to Jervase Helwyse that he should enter. The poor lunatic, it seems probable, had cherished a delusion that his haughty mistress sat in state, unharmed herself by the pestilential influence, which, as by enchantment, she scattered round about her. He dreamed, no doubt, that her beauty was not dimmed, but brightened into superhuman splendor. With such anticipations, he stole reverentially to the door at which the physician stood, but paused upon the threshold, gazing fearfully into the gloom of the darkened chamber.

"Where is the Lady Eleanore?" whispered he.

" Call her," replied the physician.

" Lady Eleanore! — Princess! — Queen of Death!" cried Jervase Helwyse, advancing three steps into the chamber. " She is not here! There, on yonder table, I behold the sparkle of a diamond which once she wore upon her bosom. There," — and he shuddered, — " there hangs her mantle, on which a dead woman embroidered a spell of dreadful potency. But where is the Lady Eleanore?"

Something stirred within the silken curtains of a canopied bed; and a low moan was uttered, which, listening intently, Jervase Helwyse began to distinguish as a woman's voice, complaining dolefully of thirst. He fancied, even, that he recognized its tones.

" My throat! — my throat is scorched," murmured the voice. " A drop of water!"

" What thing art thou?" said the brain-stricken youth, drawing near the bed and tearing asunder its curtains. " Whose voice hast thou stolen for thy murmurs and miserable petitions, as if Lady Eleanore could be conscious of mortal infirmity? Fie! Heap of diseased mortality, why lurkest thou in my lady's chamber?"

" O Jervase Helwyse," said the voice, — and, as it spoke, the figure contorted itself, struggling to hide its blasted face, — " look not now on the woman you once loved! The curse of Heaven hath stricken me, because I would not call man my brother, nor woman sister. I wrapped myself in PRIDE as in a MANTLE, and scorned the sympathies of nature; and therefore has nature made this wretched body the medium of a dreadful sympathy. You are avenged, — they are all avenged, — nature is avenged, — for I am Eleanore Rochcliffe!"

The malice of his mental disease, the bitterness lurking at
the bottom of his heart, mad as he was, for a blighted and
ruined life, and love that had been paid with cruel scorn, awoke
within the breast of Jervase Helwyse.   He shook his finger at

What Ailes Me Now!

the wretched girl, and the chamber echoed, the curtains of the
bed were shaken, with his outburst of insane merriment.

"Another triumph for the Lady Eleanore!" he cried.   "All
have been her victims!   Who so worthy to be the final victim
as herself?"

Impelled by some new fantasy of his crazed intellect, he snatched the fatal mantle and rushed from the chamber and the house. That night, a procession passed, by torchlight, through the streets, bearing in the midst the figure of a woman, enveloped with a richly embroidered mantle; while in advance stalked Jervase Helwyse, waving the red flag of the pestilence. Arriving opposite the Province House, the mob burned the effigy, and a strong wind came and swept away the ashes. It was said that, from that very hour, the pestilence abated, as if its sway had some mysterious connection, from the first plague-stroke to the last, with Lady Eleanore's Mantle. A remarkable uncertainty broods over that unhappy lady's fate. There is a belief, however, that, in a certain chamber of this mansion, a female form may sometimes be duskily discerned, shrinking into the darkest corner, and muffling her face within an embroidered mantle. Supposing the legend true, can this be other than the once proud Lady Eleanore?

Mine host, and the old loyalist, and I bestowed no little warmth of applause upon this narrative, in which we had all been deeply interested; for the reader can scarcely conceive how unspeakably the effect of such a tale is heightened when, as in the present case, we may repose perfect confidence in the veracity of him who tells it. For my own part, knowing how scrupulous is Mr. Tiffany to settle the foundation of his facts, I could not have believed him one whit the more faithfully had he professed himself an eye-witness of the doings and sufferings of poor Lady Eleanore. Some sceptics, it is true, might demand documentary evidence, or even require him to produce the embroidered mantle, forgetting that — Heaven be praised — it was

consumed to ashes.   But now the old loyalist, whose blood was
warmed by the good cheer, began to talk, in his turn, about the
traditions of the Province House, and hinted that he, if it were
agreeable, might add a few reminiscences to our legendary stock.
Mr. Tiffany, having no cause to dread a rival, immediately besought him to favor us with a specimen ; my own entreaties, of
course, were urged to the same effect ; and our venerable guest,
well pleased to find willing auditors, awaited only the return of
Mr. Thomas Waite, who had been summoned forth to provide
accommodations for several new arrivals.   Perchance the public
— but be this as its own caprice and ours shall settle the matter
— may read the result in another Tale of the Province House.

Old Esther Dudley.

IV.

OLD ESTHER DUDLEY.

OUR host having resumed the chair, he, as well as Mr.
Tiffany and myself, expressed much eagerness to be
made acquainted with the story to which the loyalist had
alluded. That venerable man first of all saw fit to moisten his
throat with another glass of wine, and then, turning his face
towards our coal fire, looked steadfastly for a few moments into
the depths of its cheerful glow. Finally, he poured forth a great
fluency of speech. The generous liquid that he had imbibed,
while it warmed his age-chilled blood, likewise took off the chill
from his heart and mind, and gave him an energy to think and
feel, which we could hardly have expected to find beneath the
snows of fourscore winters. His feelings, indeed, appeared to
me more excitable than those of a younger man ; or, at least, the
same degree of feeling manifested itself by more visible effects
than if his judgment and will had possessed the potency of meri-
dian life. At the pathetic passages of his narrative, he readily
melted into tears. When a breath of indignation swept across
his spirit, the blood flushed his withered visage even to the roots
of his white hair; and he shook his clinched fist at the trio of
peaceful auditors, seeming to fancy enemies in those who felt
very kindly towards the desolate old soul. But ever and anon,
sometimes in the midst of his most earnest talk, this ancient
person's intellect would wander vaguely, losing its hold of the

matter in hand, and groping for it amid misty shadows.   Then would he cackle forth a feeble laugh, and express a doubt whether his wits — for by that phrase it pleased our ancient friend to signify his mental powers — were not getting a little the worse for wear.

Under these disadvantages, the old loyalist's story required more revision to render it fit for the public eye than those of the series which have preceded it ; nor should it be concealed that the sentiment and tone of the affair may have undergone some slight, or perchance more than slight metamorphosis, in its transmission to the reader through the medium of a thorough-going democrat.   The tale itself is a mere sketch, with no involution of plot, nor any great interest of events, yet possessing, if I have rehearsed it aright, that pensive influence over the mind, which the shadow of the old Province House flings upon the loiterer in its courtyard.

The hour had come — the hour of defeat and humiliation — when Sir William Howe was to pass over the threshold of the Province House, and embark, with no such triumphal ceremonies as he once promised himself, on board the British fleet.   He bade his servants and military attendants go before him, and lingered a moment in the loneliness of the mansion, to quell the fierce emotions that struggled in his bosom as with a death-throb. Preferable, then, would he have deemed his fate had a warrior's death left him a claim to the narrow territory of a grave, within the soil which the king had given him to defend.   With an ominous perception that, as his departing footsteps echoed adown the staircase, the sway of Britain was passing forever from New England, he smote his clinched hand on his brow, and cursed the destiny that had flung the shame of a dismembered empire upon him.

" Would to God," cried he, hardly repressing his tears of rage, " that the rebels were even now at the doorstep! A blood-stain upon the floor should then bear testimony that the last British ruler was faithful to his trust."

The tremulous voice of a woman replied to his exclamation.

" Heaven's cause and the King's are one," it said. " Go forth, Sir William Howe, and trust in Heaven to bring back a royal governor in triumph."

Subduing at once the passion to which he had yielded only in the faith that it was unwitnessed, Sir William Howe became conscious that an aged woman, leaning on a gold-headed staff, was standing betwixt him and the door. It was old Esther Dudley, who had dwelt almost immemorial years in this mansion, until her presence seemed as inseparable from it as the recollections of its history. She was the daughter of an ancient and once eminent family, which had fallen into poverty and decay, and left its last descendant no resource save the bounty of the king, nor any shelter except within the walls of the Province House. An office in the household, with merely nominal duties, had been assigned to her as a pretext for the payment of a small pension, the greater part of which she expended in adorning herself with an antique magnificence of attire. The claims of Esther Dudley's gentle blood were acknowledged by all the successive governors; and they treated her with the punctilious courtesy which it was her foible to demand, not always with success, from a neglectful world. The only actual share which she assumed in the business of the mansion was to glide through its passages and public chambers, late at night, to see

. that the servants had dropped no fire from their flaring torches, nor left embers crackling and blazing on the hearths. Perhaps it was this invariable custom of walking her rounds in the hush of midnight that caused the superstition of the times to invest the old woman with attributes of awe and mystery; fabling that she had entered the portal of the Province House, none knew whence, in the train of the first royal governor, and that it was her fate to dwell there till the last should have departed. But Sir William Howe, if he ever heard this legend, had forgotten it.

"Mistress Dudley, why are you loitering here?" asked he, with some severity of tone. "It is my pleasure to be the last in this mansion of the king."

"Not so, if it please your Excellency," answered the time-stricken woman. "This roof has sheltered me long. I will not pass from it until they bear me to the tomb of my forefathers. What other shelter is there for old Esther Dudley, save the Province House or the grave?"

"Now Heaven forgive me!" said Sir William Howe to himself. "I was about to leave this wretched old creature to starve or beg. Take this, good Mistress Dudley," he added, putting a purse into her hands. "King George's head on these golden guineas is sterling yet, and will continue so, I warrant you, even should the rebels crown John Hancock their king. That purse will buy a better shelter than the Province House can now afford."

"While the burden of life remains upon me, I will have no other shelter than this roof," persisted Esther Dudley, striking her staff upon the floor, with a gesture that expressed immovable resolve. "And when your Excellency returns in triumph, I will totter into the porch to welcome you."

"Heaven's cause and the King's are one"

"My poor old friend!" answered the British General; and all his manly and martial pride could no longer restrain a gush of bitter tears. "This is an evil hour for you and me. The province which the king intrusted to my charge is lost. I go hence in misfortune — perchance in disgrace — to return no more. And you, whose present being is incorporated with the past, — who have seen governor after governor, in stately pageantry, ascend these steps, — whose whole life has been an observance of majestic ceremonies, and a worship of the king, — how will you endure the change? Come with us! Bid farewell to a land that has shaken off its allegiance, and live still under a royal government, at Halifax."

"Never, never!" said the pertinacious old dame. "Here will I abide; and King George shall still have one true subject in his disloyal province."

"Beshrew the old fool!" muttered Sir William Howe, growing impatient of her obstinacy, and ashamed of the emotion into which he had been betrayed. "She is the very moral of old-fashioned prejudice, and could exist nowhere but in this musty edifice. Well, then, Mistress Dudley, since you will needs tarry, I give the Province House in charge to you. Take this key, and keep it safe until myself, or some other royal governor, shall demand it of you."

Smiling bitterly at himself and her, he took the heavy key of the Province House, and, delivering it into the old lady's hands, drew his cloak around him for departure. As the General glanced back at Esther Dudley's antique figure, he deemed her well fitted for such a charge, as being so perfect a representative of the decayed past, — of an age gone by, with its manners, opinions, faith, and feelings, all fallen into oblivion or scorn, — of what had once been a reality, but was now merely a vision of faded magnificence.   Then Sir William Howe strode forth, smiting his clinched hands together, in the fierce anguish of his spirit; and old Esther Dudley was left to keep watch in

Take this key and keep it safe.

the lonely Province House, dwelling there with memory; and if Hope ever seemed to flit around her, still it was Memory in disguise.

The total change of affairs that ensued on the departure of the British troops did not drive the venerable lady from her stronghold.   There was not, for many years afterwards, a governor of Massachusetts; and the magistrates, who had charge of such matters, saw no objection to Esther Dudley's residence in the Province House, especially as they must otherwise have paid a hireling for taking care of the premises, which with her was a labor of love. And so they left her, the undisturbed mistress of the old historic edifice. Many and strange were the fables which the gossips whispered about her, in all the chimney-corners of the town. Among the time-worn articles of furniture that had been left in the mansion, there was a tall, antique mirror, which was well worthy of a tale by itself, and perhaps may hereafter be the theme of one. The gold of its heavily wrought frame was tarnished, and its surface so blurred that the old woman's figure, whenever she paused before it, looked indistinct and ghost-like. But it was the general belief that Esther could cause the governors of the overthrown dynasty, with the beautiful ladies who had once adorned their festivals, the Indian chiefs who had come up to the Province House to hold council or swear allegiance, the grim provincial warriors, the severe clergymen, — in short, all the pageantry of gone days, — all the figures that ever swept across the broad plate of glass in former times, — she could cause the whole to re-appear, and people the inner world of the mirror with shadows of old life. Such legends as these, together with the singularity of her isolated existence, her age, and the infirmity that each added winter flung upon her, made Mistress Dudley the object both of fear and pity; and it was partly the result of either sentiment that, amid all the angry license of the times, neither wrong nor insult ever fell upon her unprotected head. Indeed, there was so much haughtiness in her demeanor towards intruders, among whom she reckoned all persons acting under the new authorities, that it was really an affair of no small nerve to look her in the face. And to do the people justice, stern republicans as they had now become, they were well content that the old gentlewoman, in her hoop petticoat and faded embroidery, should still haunt the palace of ruined pride and overthrown power, the symbol of a departed system, embodying a history in her person. So Esther Dudley dwelt, year after year, in the Province House, still reverencing all that others had flung aside, still faithful to her king, who, so long as the venerable dame yet held her post, might be said to retain one true subject in New England, and one spot of the empire that had been wrested from him.

And did she dwell there in utter loneliness? Rumor said, not so. Whenever her chill and withered heart desired warmth, she was wont to summon a black slave of Governor Shirley's from the blurred mirror, and send him in search of guests who had long ago been familiar in those deserted chambers. Forth went the sable messenger, with the starlight or the moonshine gleaming through him, and did his errand in the burial-ground, knocking at the iron doors of tombs, or upon the marble slabs that covered them, and whispering to those within, " My mistress, old Esther Dudley, bids you to the Province House at midnight." And punctually as the clock of the Old South told twelve came the shadows of the Olivers, the Hutchinsons, the Dudleys, all the grandees of a bygone generation, gliding beneath the portal into the well-known mansion, where Esther mingled with them as if she likewise were a shade. Without vouching for the truth of such traditions, it is certain that Mistress Dudley sometimes assembled a few of the stanch, though crestfallen old Tories who had lingered in the rebel town during those days of wrath and tribulation. Out of a cobwebbed bottle, containing liquor that a royal governor might have smacked his lips over, they quaffed healths to the king, and

A few of the stanch, though crestfallen, old tories

babbled treason to the Republic, feeling as if the protecting shadow of the throne were still flung around them. But, draining the last drops of their liquor, they stole timorously homeward, and answered not again if the rude mob reviled them in the street.

Yet Esther Dudley's most frequent and favored guests were the children of the town. Towards them she was never stern. A kindly and loving nature, hindered elsewhere from its free course by a thousand rocky prejudices, lavished itself upon these little ones. By bribes of gingerbread of her own making, stamped with a royal crown, she tempted their sunny sportiveness beneath the gloomy portal of the Province House, and would often beguile them to spend a whole play-day there, sitting in a circle round the verge of her hoop petticoat, greedily attentive to her stories of a dead world. And when these little boys and girls stole forth again from the dark, mysterious mansion, they went bewildered, full of old feelings that graver people had long ago forgotten, rubbing their eyes at the world around them as if they had gone astray into ancient times, and become children of the past. At home, when their parents asked where they had loitered such a weary while, and with whom they had been at play, the children would talk of all the departed worthies of the province, as far back as Governor Belcher, and the haughty dame of Sir William Phipps. It would seem as though they had been sitting on the knees of these famous personages, whom the grave had hidden for half a century, and had toyed with the embroidery of their rich waistcoats, or roguishly pulled the long curls of their flowing wigs. " But Governor Belcher has been dead this many a year," would the mother say to her little boy. " And did you really see him at the Province House?" " Oh, yes, dear mother!

yes ! " the half-dreaming child would answer. " But when old Esther had done speaking about him he faded away out of his chair." Thus, without affrighting her little guests, she led them by the hand into the chambers of her own desolate heart, and made childhood's fancy discern the ghosts that haunted there.

Living so continually in her own circle of ideas, and never regulating her mind by a proper reference to present things, Esther Dudley appears to have grown partially crazed. It was found that she had no right sense of the progress and true state of the Revolutionary War, but held a constant faith that the armies of Britain were victorious on every field, and destined to be ultimately triumphant. Whenever the town rejoiced for a battle won by Washington, or Gates, or Morgan, or Greene, the news, in passing through the door of the Province House, as through the ivory gate of dreams, became metamorphosed into a strange tale of the prowess of Howe, Clinton, or Cornwallis. Sooner or later, it was her invincible belief, the colonies would be prostrate at the footstool of the king. Sometimes she seemed to take for granted that such was already the case. On one occasion she startled the townspeople by a brilliant illumination of the Province House, with candles at every pane of glass, and a transparency of the king's initials and a crown of light in the great balcony window. The figure of the aged woman, in the most gorgeous of her mildewed velvets and brocades, was seen passing from casement to casement, until she paused before the balcony, and flourished a huge key above her head. Her wrinkled visage actually gleamed with triumph, as if the soul within her were a festal lamp.

" What means this blaze of light ? What does old Esther's joy portend ? " whispered a spectator. " It is frightful to see her gliding about the chambers, and rejoicing there without a soul to bear her company."

"It is as if she were making merry in a tomb," said another.

"Pshaw! It is no such mystery," observed an old man, after some brief exercise of memory. "Mistress Dudley is keeping jubilee for the King of England's birthday." Then the people laughed aloud, and would have thrown mud against the blazing transparency of the king's crown and initials, only that they pitied the poor old dame, who was so dismally triumphant amid the wreck and ruin of the system to which she appertained.

The King of England's birth-day -

Oftentimes it was her custom to climb the weary staircase that wound upward to the cupola, and thence strain her dimmed eyesight seaward and countryward, watching for a British fleet, or for the march of a grand procession, with the king's banner floating over it. The passengers in the street below would discern her anxious visage, and send up a shout, "When the golden Indian on the Province House shall shoot his arrow, and when the cock on the Old South spire shall crow, then look for a royal governor again!" — for this had grown a byword through the town. And at last, after long, long years, old Esther Dudley knew, or perchance she only dreamed, that a royal governor was on the eve of returning to the Province House, to receive the heavy key which Sir William Howe had committed to her charge. Now it was the fact that intelligence bearing some faint analogy to Esther's version of it was current among the townspeople. She set the mansion in the best order that her means allowed, and, arraying herself in silks and tarnished gold, stood long before the blurred mirror to admire her own magnificence. As she gazed, the gray and withered lady moved her ashen lips, murmuring half aloud, talking to shapes that she saw within the mirror, to shadows of her own fantasies, to the household friends of memory, and bidding them rejoice with her, and come forth to meet the governor. And, while absorbed in this communion, Mistress Dudley heard the tramp of many footsteps in the street, and, looking out at the window, beheld what she construed as the royal governor's arrival.

"O happy day! O blessed, blessed hour!" she exclaimed. "Let me but bid him welcome within the portal, and my task in the Province House, and on earth, is done!"

Then with tottering feet, which age and tremulous joy caused to tread amiss, she hurried down the grand staircase, her silks sweeping and rustling as she went, so that the sound was as if a train of spectral courtiers were thronging from the dim mirror. And Esther Dudley fancied that, as soon as the wide door should be flung open, all the pomp and splendor of bygone times would pace majestically into the Province House, and the gilded tapestry of the past would be brightened by the sunshine of the

present. She turned the key, — withdrew it from the lock, — unclosed the door, — and stepped across the threshold. Advancing up the courtyard appeared a person of most dignified mien, with tokens, as Esther interpreted them, of gentle blood, high rank, and long-accustomed authority, even in his walk and every gesture. He was richly dressed, but wore a gouty shoe, which, however, did not lessen the stateliness of his gait. Around and behind him were people in plain civic dresses, and two or three war-worn veterans, evidently officers of rank, arrayed in a uniform of blue and buff. But Esther Dudley, firm in the belief that had fastened its roots about her heart, beheld only the principal personage, and never doubted that this 'was the long-looked-for governor, to whom she was to surrender up her charge. As he approached, she involuntarily sank down on her knees, and tremblingly held forth the heavy key.

"Receive my trust! take it quickly!" cried she; "for methinks Death is striving to snatch away my triumph. But he comes too late. Thank Heaven for this blessed hour! God save King George!"

"That, madam, is a strange prayer to be offered up at such a moment," replied the unknown guest of the Province House, and, courteously removing his hat, he offered his arm to raise the aged woman. "Yet, in reverence for your gray hairs and long-kept faith, Heaven forbid that any here should say you nay. Over the realms which still acknowledge his sceptre, God save King George!"

Esther Dudley started to her feet, and, hastily clutching back the key, gazed with fearful earnestness at the stranger; and dimly and doubtfully, as if suddenly awakened from a dream, her bewildered eyes half recognized his face. Years

ago, she had known him among the gentry of the province.
But the ban of the king had fallen upon him! How, then,
came the doomed victim here? Proscribed, excluded from
mercy, the monarch's most dreaded and hated foe, this New
England merchant had stood triumphantly against a kingdom's
strength; and his foot now trod upon humbled royalty, as he
ascended the steps of the Province House, the people's chosen
governor of Massachusetts.

"Wretch, wretch that I am!" muttered the old woman,
with such a heart-broken expression that the tears gushed from
the stranger's eyes. " Have I bidden a traitor welcome? Come,
Death! come quickly! "

"Alas, venerable lady!" said Governor Hancock, lending
her his support with all the reverence that a courtier would have
shown to a queen. " Your life has been prolonged until the
world has changed around you. You have treasured up all that
time has rendered worthless, — the principles, feelings, manners, modes of being and acting, which another generation has
flung aside, — and you are a symbol of the past. And I, and
these around me, — we represent a new race of men, — living
no longer in the past, scarcely in the present, — but projecting
our lives forward into the future. Ceasing to model ourselves
on ancestral superstitions, it is our faith and principle to press
onward, onward! Yet," continued he, turning to his attendants,
" let us reverence, for the last time, the stately and gorgeous
prejudices of the tottering Past! "

While the republican governor spoke, he had continued to
support the helpless form of Esther Dudley; her weight grew
heavier against his arm; but at last, with a sudden effort to free
herself, the ancient woman sank down beside one of the pillars

of the portal. The key of the Province House fell from her grasp, and clanked against the stone.

" I have been faithful unto death," murmured she. " God save the king ! "

" She hath done her office ! " said Hancock solemnly. " We will follow her reverently to the tomb of her ancestors ; and then, my fellow-citizens, onward, — onward ! We are no longer children of the Past ! "

As the old loyalist concluded his narrative, the enthusiasm which had been fitfully flashing within his sunken eyes, and quivering across his wrinkled visage, faded away, as if all the lingering fire of his soul were extinguished. Just then, too, a lamp upon the mantel-piece threw out a dying gleam, which vanished as speedily as it shot upward, compelling our eyes to grope for one another's features by the dim glow of the hearth. With such a lingering fire, methought, with such a dying gleam, had the glory of the ancient system vanished from the Province House, when the spirit of old Esther Dudley took its flight. And now, again, the clock of the Old South threw its voice of ages on the breeze, knolling the hourly knell of the Past, crying out far and wide through the multitudinous city, and filling our ears, as we sat in the dusky chamber, with its reverberating depth of tone. In that 'same mansion, — in that very chamber, — what a volume of history had been told off into hours, by the same voice that was now trembling in the air. Many a governor had heard those midnight accents, and longed to exchange his stately cares for slumber. And as for mine host, and Mr. Bela Tiffany, and the old loyalist, and me, we had babbled about dreams of the past, until we almost fancied that the clock was still striking in a bygone century. Neither of us would have wondered had a hoop-petticoated phantom of Esther Dudley tottered into the chamber, walking her rounds in the hush of midnight, as of yore, and motioned us to quench the fading embers of the fire, and leave the historic precincts to herself and her kindred shades. But, as no such vision was vouchsafed, I retired unbidden, and would advise Mr. Tiffany to lay hold of another auditor, being resolved not to show my face in the Province House for a good while hence, — if ever.

Fa thful vnto death

www.ingramcontent.com/pod-product-compliance
Lightning Source LLC
Chambersburg PA
CBHW020411030726
47496CB00007B/2413